Spectral Serenades

Ghosts Of Phantoms Sung

By

George O. Obikoya

Without a doubt, nothing is going to make the matter vamoose: after all it does not exist. Its presumed criticalness is, therefore, not deemed a myth. This is the prevalent view after years of efforts in the community to comprehend what really happened on the school bus on the day the world appeared to slide back to pre-Copernican days, a fateful day indeed. They were only thirteen years old, too young many town folks say to do any such thing, something they insisted they did and were not remorseful about. In fact, they felt proud they did what they allegedly did. They all even said that they would do it again, if they had another chance. This was then, O yes, over a decade ago, but the matter is going nowhere in a hurry, if at all, after all it does not exist, physically that is, although not everyone in town agrees with this point of view they concur the matter is critical as it is on everyone's mind, driving folks nuts!

The prevalent view on the matter has waxed and waned over the years more so considering the vacillations of the now-twenty something year-olds whose accounts of the incident have not been consistent nor have they always been believable. In fact, some of them have even denied it ever happened, others blame their recollections of the incident on 'too much TV.' So, we have opinions with an expected spread on a matter most town folks are losing sleep over, unable to wish it away, no matter how hard they try, a situation compounded by the mysterious death of the driver of the school bus just days after the incident yea, most town folks even more inclined to believe him than anyone else involved in the matter, his account of the non-physicalness of the incident a key reason for the enduring awe it invokes and the continuing interest of the towns people in disentangling its grip.

Its intriguing complexity has become the collective angst of the townspeople, who are worried the incident may happen again, concerned that a group of teenagers may engage non-existent matters that stick in peoples' minds, the stars 'low-low,' as if Einstein must defer to Newton after all: something is pulling on something it seems, essentially forcing it to pay homage to the void, well, in a manner of speaking since the teenagers spoke and did not speak 'with one voice,' as if someone or something got them confused to get everyone else confused, given the varieties of stories related to the matter popping out of pates nearly every single day, whereas the teenagers are now more focused on their present not past lives, more so, apparently no longer rhapsodized by the popularity they enjoyed that has, over the years, turned into notoriety, the mockery they endure 'not conducive to learning.'

That is what they claim explains their poor academic performances in college; others say they are experiencing the repercussions of playing with matters that don't exist, an incident yea in a school bus that still has what many refer to as a weird stranglehold on an entire community years after it occurred, its anniversary remembered with a vigil at the site of the event every year, relic of the school bus still in the woods at the back of the town hall covered with tarpaulin, no one even sure what is now beneath the tarpaulin, more so that it looks much smaller than a school bus, yet, no one appears curious enough to want to find out, at least until recently when an office assistant at the town hall ventured near the bus, well, presumably, the bus, ostensibly accidentally, having gone into the woods to 'meditate' after work, but fled the area in a panic when the 'bus' began to glow.

News of this latest encounter with what does not exist regarding the bus yea only further
heightened the townspeople's conviction that there is something mysterious going on yea in their
community, something quite scary, even ominous, something that seems to defy logic set
Newton against Einstein, something seemingly Pre-Copernican, the town, the epicenter of
an unexplainable 'gravitational pull' of matters that do not exist, yet entertained
teenagers-turned backseat school bus drivers: the driver was 'unresponsive' yet obeyed the 'bosses''
instructions and drove the teens round town when in fact the bus never left the school grounds, not even for
a second throughout what the teens, grown, described as an hour-long jape of orgiastic revelry,
apparently in gossamery with bacchanalian company, an incongruity that's
a looking glass as folks struggle to grasp the weirdness of life in a town of glaring opposites.

So, 'nothingness' continues to make sense as nothing else does, 'quantum gravity' does not thrill, no
attempt at a 'unified theory' to explain the universe does; no tests helps to debunk
the notion of the speed of light slowing, worse still, another of the so-called nature's constants may
also become 'inconstant' any time soon, and school buses may start glowing even on the streets,
our void, tilting perilously on its pivot in a remote town in the middle of nowhere
perhaps a gate, who knows? O well, maybe folks that claim to have had encounters with aliens did,
after all, they describe a wide range of weird, 'unnatural' experiences with these often
weird-looking entities, including orgiastic ones, entities we may say do not exist,
that we may refer to as ghostly entities yet able to abduct non-ghostly entities
sex them up to breed babies; did someone say nephilims? So, folks do the babies exist and don't?

Yes, we remember Schrödinger's cat, you know, dead and alive at once while we try to figure what
to do re the 'measurement problem,' yes, figure if and how a random subatomic event,
a 'wavefunction collapse,' when a superimposition of different eigenstates, referred to
yea as a wavefunction becomes one eigenstate upon interacting with the 'observer' or
'measurer,' with the material or existent world, occurred, what we did to turn what does not
exist, in the physical sense that is, into what exists, a glowing bus yes from some spectral
event for example, or courtesy calls from nephilims, or from quantized virtual photons,
so folks, we may 'conjure' and command entities that do not exist as Solomon did in the
olden days and, by the way, can we then blame God for the evils of the world? Did God let evil
happen? Folks, we will address these important questions atheists like to ask later, in some form O yea.

For now, we mull the measurement problem, we ponder the matter of the what does not exist yea
popping everywhere in a voided space, and wonder, we wonder if even only nothingness
flowers in our minds, surrounded as we are encircled by transitioning entities herein
shaping reshaping, shifting in and out of void in a seemingly effortless manner that has
us wondering what is really going on in this voided space, asking where all the ghosts are, yes
pondering our mysterious world, wherein shimmering amorphousnesses mingle in the mall,
with assorted heads, one in which school buses become bacchanal suites glowing in the woods, on the
highways, in the streets, everywhere you look a veritable catacomb of anamorphic states
emulating ghosts, everybody dead, carrions on stilts herein motorized with a tiny
cell of codified spells, a heart non-existent in existent mattered states cheering for a snake.

We wonder what ghosts are to start with wonder where they are, and how they seem able to manifest
herein in our voided space, as apparitions as some people say, or hallucinations as

some others hold, things that are not existent seen as existent, you know, a pathological
state to some requiring treatment with drugs, maybe with a little magic mushroom in pill forms or
with a lung-full of hashish 'pro re nata' yea, to ensure those nuisances never pop up here
again unannounced, you know, un-conjured, which highlights the issue of whether or not these phantoms,
these spectral entities are free agents or slaves under our control, after all the teens claimed they
could recreate the incident that occurred in the bus, you know, much like with a sleight of hand, just
like that; folks, isn't it nice to feel like being the boss in our void for a change? It sure is! Maybe
we really are, after all we have the 'power' to vote people here in and out of office, right?

Yes we do, something we must always bear in mind, given there are probably 'people' walking here
among us we need never vote into office or must vote out if they managed to chicane there
yes. These are serious matters folks, matters we cannot wish away, our considerations of
non-existents masquerading as existents, maneuvering their way to office only to
start creating chaos in our precious world once in office dear mates, a situation we all
cannot afford given the precariousness of the delicateness that pivots our void, yes,
making it even harder folks for us to use the window of opportunity to harness
the energy of entropy for the benefit of our inherently moribund
void, as some contend considering what entropy does, so, folks, why should we not recognize our
power and utilize it appropriately for the betterment of humanity O yea?

Book 2

Yes, folks, we have the power to modify our world, to make it a better place for everyone
of us, regardless of the existence of phantoms in our midst dear folks, which makes our efforts to
comprehend the interplay of spectral and material entities herein folks even more
interesting, in other words digging into the mechanics of the 'glowing bus' will, doubtless,
be fun, yet, it is figuring the implications of this mechanism for us and our void
that matters much more, for here we are faced with enormous challenges we do not know who or what
creates and tweaks that may be 'otherworldly' yea: we do not know if any of us controlled our
void from spectral realms dear folks, we are clueless re who or what the ghosts are herein messing with our
pates, and we need to know and want to know who or what they are, we have the right to know otherwise,
as Hobbes warned, we may be in for a life that is 'solitary, poor, nasty, brutish and short,' yes.

Sadly folks, we would have annulled our social contract, the 'sovereign' no longer able yes to
ensure that we are not reaching for one another's jugular at the slightest excuse O yes
ready to exact the proverbial 'pound of flesh' as usury reigns supreme, even Shylock
greened! Well, perhaps no one will be impressed with that since envy is normative everywhere we look,
you know, the gene for narcissism runs in almost every tot! So, what to do? Do we not try
to figure if some 'walking stick' was not a gene-tweaker, an expert geneticist here running
a spectral lab unleashing viruses in a void in experimental singularity,
you know, creating cyborgs and also sorts of weirdness in our minds? Perhaps we all ought to be
watching television in our sleep, you know, wolfing popcorns, not trying to 'solve the world's problems'
after all they are not ours; they belong to someone else in some hut in a remote location.

Yes, they are someone else's problems, right? Yeah right, until they come knocking on our doors inviting
us to the school of hard knocks, yes, run by walking sticks! Ok, let's leave the ghosts alone for now, let's
return to the question we earlier posed regarding atheists' counter argument to the
so-called 'argument by design' for the existence of God assuming, according yea to some
traditions that a supreme deity created the world, in other words, it ought not to let
evil happen and ought to be able to stop it, this notion essentially ruling out the
spectral entities we have been speculating about as being the controllers of the world, which
means these ghosts, aliens, or whatever must have also been designed by a supreme being, one that
must, as such, be held responsible for letting them unleash chaos in our voided space, more so
if we held the view of the continuum of consciousness between what exists and what does not.

Folks, can we really blame anyone but ourselves for evil in the world, even dear mates for the
'butterfly effect'? Not sure, some would probably respond, many more with an emphatic 'no'! Yes,
and with good reasons, given our role in thinning the 'ozone layer,' felling trees with yes reckless
abandon and menacing delicate ecosystems worldwide with no regard at all for the
consequences of our recklessness on climate change, to cite one instance of our atrocities
herein in our void, not to mention the wars we wage to feed the 'military-industrial
complex,' that behemoth of insatiable appetite, that Leviathan that threatens yea
to wolf us all, and so on and so forth, so we ask: what has God got to do with all that, dear mates
regardless if conceived in concrete or abstract terms? What do we all really know about God to
ascribe attributes to who or what we struggle to conceptualize let alone define?

We barely even know who we are folks! We are not even certain we are not the ghosts we call
ghosts, spiritual entities phantoms manifest, or are we, eh? With 'aliens' walking here
among us, are we? Let's face it folks, we may all simply be singing spectral songs vocalizing
herein in a void, the songs of ghosts by ghosts for ghosts, we may be ghosts entertaining or killing
ghosts: wait a second, did someone say ghosts killing ghosts entertaining ghosts herein? Lord have mercy!
There really must be something about these folks, pardon me, ghosts! Yes, something we all really ought to
want to know and must seek to know. Well, not only do 'aliens' live in our midst as some folks say,
but we are also said to be amalgams, in some traditions, you know, we are all said to be
atavistic epigenetic epiphenomena accretions on a core, a primal
core pristine corrupted in a void, by money, by greed by 'trickle-down' buffoonery O yes.

So, we can be anything we want, right? Shylocks, Merry Andrews, buffoons, knaves even insurgents,
we can be whatever we want so why blame God? After all, what God created was all good, pristine!
Folks, we must not blame God in our discourses on good and evil we must not at all invoke an
argument by design deluding ourselves we can chicane to Eden's gate, bribe Charon to fly
us across the Acheron in our 'intergalactic capsules' or in our 'teleportation
contraptions' dear mates, no we cannot bribe our way to the inter-dimensional realm, we must face
the fact that we made our bed, and we will lie on it how we did! Yes, we should be keener yea to
figure the mechanics of intergalactic realms than hexing what or who is way beyond our
grasp in inter-dimensional realms thinking we are some really smart dudes capable of telling
between walking sticks and vectors, or between erectile reptiles and bipedal ants in a mall.

It seems unfair to blame God or anyone for our foes, if even some evil appear, at least
on the surface, to be so-called 'acts of God;' blimey who says? Who says they are acts of God when they
could jolly well be acts of ghosts? The matter of what or who exists and do not exist is yes
indeed, not that complicated if only we could modify our mindsets a little bit, if
we would stop saying nothing other than the material exists, you know, dismissing ghosts, or
shall we say, dismissing the notion of the continuum of consciousness asserting yea the
incompatibility of the material and immaterial if only we would
open our minds to knowledge from eclectic sources, including those to which we are not very
accustomed O yea, may be new vistas would emerge and the prospects of the material and
the immaterial being along a continuum no longer in doubt, to wit: A key shift!

Yes, it would be a paradigm shift, Kuhn likely turning in his grave: we cannot gainsay yea the
significance of its influence on discourses dear mates, so, we must not underrate yea its
potential impact on each and everyone of us and for our world herein, yes, we are all now
able to talk about ghosts more freely with no scientist chiding us, our views on those 'glowing'
buses will now be more nuanced, we will no longer be aporetic throw our hands up in the
air folks, demoralized at not being able to 'discover,' those entities we believe are in
our midst we call elves, entities prancing in our pates tormenting us in void, their ilks spreading bad
vibes herein in our space 'experimenting' with all sorts of things including prions, viruses, yes
whatever yes using humans as 'hosts,' messing with our heads fooling around with our precious void,
yes folks, we would be on the right track at last, on track to better comprehend ourselves and our world.

At last, folks, hopefully, after all Newton and Leibniz were occultists, you know, they were not yea
averse to the notion of ghosts, and Descartes had this evil genius to solidify his

argument that our senses are not reliable knowledge sources yes, a quintessential
rationalist he was a thorn in the flesh of empiricists in his days, perhaps he still is
even now, some would argue, his epistemological doubt rendering yes the distinction
between the material and immaterial, irrelevant, it appears. In any case,
it is unlikely the most 'ideological' that will likely yea consider themselves pure
rationalists or empiricists these days 'glowing' school buses cruising on city streets herein
folks in a voided space even in the woods and on the highways must be telling us something yes,
perhaps that aliens are behind the wheels, even in limousines, that ghost are everywhere, yes.

We must forge ahead unfazed dear mates open our minds to issues herein matters that may not or
may exist engender in our precious world, that we may be receptive yea to notions herein
that may assist us in our bid to better figure ourselves and our world dear mates, a task we all
cannot and must not neglect let alone ignore, lest be overwhelmed by forces we may not at
all even know are here planning to destroy our world exploiting the zombified folks we have all
become incessantly pounded with information to dumb us down, grand narratives of all sorts
to condition us to think and act in certain ways under certain circumstances dear mates, all
sorts of mind control tactics visited on us be it 'subliminal' or kro-kro eye as some
would say: Lord have mercy! So, who or what is doing these things to us and why? Who needs herein to
control us keep us in Platonic caves chasing 'shadows' in the dark O yea, who or what, by Jove?

Book 3

What is really going on herein in our void? This is one question that may be on every lip
but one that no one may be able to answer with certainty yea, more so regarding folks the
pervasive so-called 'human condition' and its resultant angst that keep us all in chains yes, in
other words, why would anyone want to create a 'human condition' which, essentially
translates to poverty, material and immaterial, or put differently O yes,
physical and spiritual poverty that engenders an existential angst, whereas
Descartes' evil genius must have us wondering who or what is doing the doubting hence yea
thinking, as such, purporting they exist, more so given our position on us being amalgams,
yes, given the Trinitarian doctrine in some traditions and the belief in other such
multi-entity beings prevalent in cultures worldwide, really, who, or what it is tweaking void?

Is it something that must manifest in a physical form in void or, as in some traditions,
a spirit here in a physical form, which latter belies its 'continuum-ness,' O yes, its
'physical-ness' in its ability to exist in a material form many would say,
self-evident here in void, a testament to the link between the spiritual and yea the
physical? The continuum of consciousness may indeed be evident but not, we may say,
necessary yea that this something must manifest in a physical form in void, nor does it
mean that the physical form must manifest as a spiritual form, assuming it could mates
manifest anywhere along the continuum of consciousness we have identified, which
suggests that matters that exist, that manifest in physical form, what we customarily
mean by saying something exists, may also not exist yet 'exists,' herein in our void, O yes.

Folks, we may sound tautological here but we are making an important distinction between
existence in different states within the same intergalactic realm, the realm where ghosts and yea
'humans' operate in tandem O yea, our notion of humans not mainstream, if even widely
held in different versions, such as with the Trinitarian doctrine, in sundry cultures yea,
which tells us that we are not the only ones that talk about us being amalgams folks, peoples all
over the void do not toss the point that amalgams, ghosts, humans, whatever we call us exist,
after all, it changes nothing about the fact that someone or something is 'doing' something, yea
'thinking' that is, which in Cartesian parlance implies they must exist, regardless physical
or spiritual, material or immaterial, a fact that O yes has serious
implications for our approaches to elucidating void, figuring out ourselves.

Yes, for we may just be the ghosts we are looking for, whether or not we like to admit to this
potential truth which supports Descartes contention that reason trumps experience, our senses, yea
unreliable sources of gen, so, there we go again folks, locked in the rationalism
versus empiricism conundrum, when folks, we ought to be mulling the intergalactic
entities walking in our midst creating chaos in our voided space, aware that there may be
other entities that are benevolent rather than malevolent towards us, why we must
take these matters very seriously and do our best to understand ourselves that we may yea
understand our world, that whatever is controlling us may realize it's time they stopped taking
us for a ride, treating us as slaves, messing with our pates, yes, folks, we must want to know whatever
we need to know to free ourselves from bondage at last, after all, we may just be the slave owners.

We have made this point earlier and will make it again from time to time since we are trying to
make no qualitative distinctions between ghosts other than concerning morphology, there being
innumerable forms of intergalactic entities that all share the common feature of
being intergalactic entities, albeit of varying abilities, just as we do,
yea to affect other entities, in a variety of ways dear folks, materially or
physically and immaterially or spiritually: we have made the point that we
may be the ghosts we are searching for, the entities controlling us herein in a void, yes, we
may need to look no farther than our intergalactic realm and stop hexing God for our 'doing'
including our 'thinking' and our 'acting' that give us the confidence that we indeed exist, so,
folks, let's combine this with our experiences here and see what we get: material or what?

Doubtless, we are familiar with the varieties of human behavior, good or bad, we are
accustomed to the tendencies of people to pass the buck, kick the can down the road and yes to
engage in unconscionable or in kind acts we have grown to considering humans as flawed
and some folks blame God for poor workmanship creating us to be so flawed, folks, not to mention for
allowing evil to exist in void, whereas we may be the ones to blame for our foes and, for
that matter, the ones to receive credit for our good deeds. We are unlikely to make much progress
figuring out ourselves dear mates comprehending void if we did not open up our minds to these
possibilities O yea, something that may be harder to achieve than we think because of the
very nature of the amalgams we are, over which countless intergalactic entities
or, shall we say, consciousnesses, constantly vie for hegemony, for control over something.

Yes, over something in us, something we hitherto suggested is money, which is dear mates yea,
information, which is energy, yes energy, so folks, these countless entities being O yes,
intergalactic may manifest anywhere along the continuum of consciousness here
manifest or not in void as they jostle for control over the vanquished yea, typically
including us one could argue, hitherto, was due to the extent of the control they have yea
over money, you know, over energy, the more of which begot even more, you know, further
impoverishing the vanquished into a cycle of further impoverishment, a cycle
we are determined to break! Yes, folks, we are not going to let these so-called victors take any
more energy away from us for a bowl of rice, which is what this whole nonsense amounts to yes,
a 'Policy of Encirclement' perpetrated on individuals, even countries, yes.

Dear mates, yes, deprived of our means of livelihood even simply being citizens of a country,
we are trapped in a cycle of poverty and chaos that makes us vulnerable herein to
capitulating to these demonic entities and opening the door for them to exact
even more money from whatever else we have in our coffers and, by the way, the smaller we
are the easier for this evil control scheme to work with devastating effects, so, we end
up empowering the already empowered as we grind in slavery for aye, this is the
cycle of injustice going on in our void we are determined to stop by voting out its
perpetrators at the ballot box. We will not let money beget even more yea at our own
expense: money, no matter how many bowls of rice we are offered, will not determine who we
will or will not vote for forthwith, we will vote according to our consciences yea, we will be free.

Indeed, we will be free, we will defeat our foes mates at the polls for we are forging ahead yes

comprehending the shenanigans of the countless intergalactic entities herein yea
operating in our voided space using our energy to sustain themselves at our expense,
for what else is one percent looking for grabbing eighty percent or more of the void's wealth leaving
the remaining ninety-nine percent of us in the lurch? Think about it folks, there must be more than
meets the eye regarding this issue and it is important for us to get to the bottom of
how much energy, for instance, an entity even needs to sustain itself, you know, yea to
survive, as we are not privy to these characters sleeping on eleven beds combined at night
or wolfing a bucket-full of rice hiding in their closets in the dead of night! Whatever they
are doing with the money, or information, or energy must be revealed, folks, let's be free.

We must be free to vote for or against who we choose. Let us no longer be afraid of ghosts like
us, we must not be intimidated by the stage-managed so-called human condition that our
so-called controllers have institutionalized through countless strategies and tactics of social
control, more so, through misinformation and information asymmetry, forms of energy
manipulation that put more energy in the hands of those entities yea, operating
cryptically or in broad daylight, determined to perpetually enslave us all yes, no
matter knights or knaves we are, so, let us open our eyes and dump all the grand narratives herein
dumped on us by dubious sources of gen calculated to keep us dumbed down for aye by those
con artists that preach 'prosperity' stupidness and shamelessly flaunt their private jets and limos
in our noses to smell the skunk they truly are. Our world has changed folks, smelly aliens here, yes!

Book 4

Yes, folks, we seem to have heartless consciousnesses lurking herein in our midst, and they do not at
all yes appear to have any good intentions toward us. Let us not kid ourselves fighting one
another when we have a common enemy determined it appears, to do us all in O
yes render us extinct, for what does one call what a virus is doing these days in our void? What
do we say about whatever has the power to control our world that we must not even think,
it seems, may have a hand in a virus ravaging our world which, if it didn't kill us left us
with unaffordable medical bills that so scares us folks we no longer even go to the
emergency room, has us essentially waiting to die of whatever else? What should Sue,
a retired engineer who has now lost her sight unable to afford appointments with her eye
doctor and has over ten thousand dollars in credit card debts due to medical bills, think about ghosts?

Folks, what is she supposed to think about her social contract, or the Leviathan, or about
an ouroboros yes the beast, so-called 'bosses,' the externalized hierarchy? Meanwhile, we
are hearing that the 'virus' was 'manufactured' in some lab! In some lab in a fish market in
the East funded by some folks in the West! Talk about Tolstoy in New York! So, why should we folks not talk
about 'us,' whatever or whoever 'us' comprises, being the ones doing ourselves in? Why must
we not talk about who or what holds sway in the amalgams that we all are, more when someone or
something and its legislator-allies seem to be so afraid of the people they panic just
hearing the 'p' word, they are so terrified of the people that hundreds of voter-suppression
legislations under their auspices are sprouting like some lunatic weeds everywhere we look?
O well, may God save them from themselves, Amen. Let's talk about our stories folks, serenade for void.

Indeed, let us celebrate life and not be fodders for bugs. Did someone say fodders? Well, maybe
we are fodder thinking we are not, yet, we may be dancing to the music of our predators
seeing ourselves only as physical beings, a notion that some people ballyhoo as sine
qua non to consciousness, in other words, affirming consciousness requires the existence yes of
a physical being, that it is only a physical being that can experience consciousness.
These 'researchers' go as far as to ascribe certain attributes such as structure, integration
and exclusivity to consciousness, denying yea the possibility herein of an
amalgamated consciousness for instance, their argument Descartes will unlikely even care
to refute as it predicates on experience, an empiricist's world view he declared yes
unreliable, which we, even now, cannot contend, so, folks, we refuse to be fodders.

We are not fodders serenading life, celebrating existence in whatever form along
yes the continuum of consciousness we may be, material or otherwise, dear folks, our
nimbleness our strength, what makes us able to outsmart or at least favourably compete here with
other entities in the information marketplace, and to not be mere fodders to be kicked
about by any 'alien visitor' with or without a bogus deal, which underscores the
importance of our approaches to conceptualizing and elucidating consciousness
for figuring the issues that confront us herein in a void, you know, those glowing school buses
those walking sticks those shimmering amorphousnesses those vectors, erectile reptiles and what nots!
Yes, for better understanding the so-called visitors creating chaos in our void O yes,
why we must continue to see consciousness as an amalgam of consciousnesses herein, yes.

So, our search for the constituents of an amalgam and quest for understanding herein its
mechanics continue for, unlike the empiricist, we believe we can O yes decompose
consciousness to whatever level, guess what, in the intergalactic realm herein, yea in the
material-immaterial realm of humans and walking sticks, which folks makes the notion of
materiality being necessary and sufficient for consciousness to exist, a view
incompatible with that of a decomposable consciousness yea but also dear mates self-
contradictory rooting consciousness in physicality, in 'Experience,' yes in the
senses in unreliability, a view ours of the interplay or experience and
reason in the foundations of consciousness does not fit. Folks, we must not fool ourselves thinking our
brain has all the answers we seek regarding this mysterious world of ours wherein werewolves game.

We must not forget our folks that coronavirus has killed and the loved ones they left behind, we
must remember all the brave soldiers that lost their lives or were wounded in the wars waged all around
the world for reasons that may be just as cryptic as their perpetrators are, war mongers funding
both sides of the wars at once! Yes, let memories of the victims of racism, bigotry, hate,
xenophobia, genocide and all the other atrocities herein that 'humans' committed
against humanity be fresh in our minds dear mates, yea, let us be determined to ensure no
one suppresses our votes, that no one denies us our fundamental right to cast our vote yea for
whoever we choose, after all we stand by the ideal that we hold the truth that we are all born
equal to be self-evident, as we do that democracy is sacrosanct and that the more
of us participate in it the better will be our world: let's not let anyone ruin it.

We must not allow the enemies of democracy to prevail in void, we must not tire folks
trying to figure who or what these 'humans' really are and what they want from us herein in our
space, our very special void. That we are even looking for aliens in our midst suggests we
think they have different physical attributes than us but they are not standing out in the mall,
or on the city streets or anywhere in void: if not why are we still looking for them herein,
as Fermi's paradox implies? What does it mean to the empiricist, by the way, that there is
an ongoing investigation ordered by senior lawmakers O yes in a spacefaring-
pioneer nation regarding unidentified aerial phenomena? Balderdash eh?
C'mon folks, is someone being left behind that really ought to know that Maxwell of the 'second great
unification in physics' fame, had a 'demon' yes, a demon in his thought experiment?

O yes, folks, a demon that violated the second law of thermodynamics, creating
an 'issue' in physics, an issue re our ideas on entropy that continues yes till
today in the discourses on the connections herein between information theory and
the laws that govern the links between different forms of energy, the measurability
of which, at the macro-level as physical quantities and explainability of their
behavior re energy distribution among their minutest constituents O yea with
statistical mechanics is instructive herein regarding, dear mates, the idea yes of
'materiality in immateriality,' yes, our considerations confined to
the intergalactic realm, considerations that put not just the hard boiled empiricists but
also the so-called cryptic entities that control our void instantly under the kliegs O yes.

Something which, by the way, appears these entities detest, well, who likes to wash their dirty linens
in public, more washed for them unsolicited if not actively discouraged maltreating yea

journalists and anyone else even contemplating any such 'dastardly' acts? The point though
is that we don't have to read what we don't want to read, an undeniably sound advice some folks
may not be interested to know let alone follow given their hidden agenda for the
human race, one that is unlikely to be benevolent if it must be secreted yes in
a voided space, regardless, we reserve the right to know what is going on in our world dear mates,
we ought to want to know whatever we can regarding the mechanics of our very precious
world, we want to know if some hidden heads really operate in the shadows presented to us
yea in our catacombs herein the Platonic caves in which we dwell as reality O yes.

Don't we folks? That something is awry here in our void that may imperil us all folks we must not
deny, more so that it may just be some matter that does not exist but indeed exists, you
know, some cat! Did someone say cat? Well, we may be dealing with a snake, a spider, or any form
of matter at that immaterial laid, imperceptible to the naked eye, or so it
seems, given that the nearness or otherwise of the imperceptible to perception counts, not
to mention the observer's perceptual abilities being perhaps extra-sensory or
something like that, so folks, the hidden may in fact be hidden in plain sight or not at all for some
observers dear mates: imagine how uncomfortable that might make the 'masked' ones feel! Verily
we may say, quite so. Yet, we do not set out to make anyone feel uncomfortable, we just
want to understand our void to better make our very precious world for the good of all, O yes.

Book 5

S o, folks we will not relent in our efforts to explore our void, to elucidate the workings
of the ghosts we are that manifest yea in Jack and Jill expressing sundry thoughts, our notion of
consciousness rooted in the interactiveness herein of aspects of an entity along
a spectrum of expressions manifest or not yea in physical forms, yes mates we want to know
how these phantoms operate, we want to venture beyond the brain to explain the brain O yea in
a bony case or that in the gut or in the heart or the mind or whatever wherever else
folks in our body and to which we, with our empiricists hat on, ascribe herein the so-called
'intelligence' that we so ballyhoo as placing us on the pedestal around which the stars
dance to spectral serenades: yes, we will and will do so within the framework upon which yes the
accretion of atavistic epigenetic epiphenomena occurs: the framework.

The framework of the amalgam that is, the atavistic 'skeleton' we all carry forward
upon which the alliances energy transactions engender accrue in entropic states
in the arrow of time, never mind what Maxwell's demon lets in or out of its gates, although we
must, who or what Mephistopheles lets out of his, if even we were not yea considering
waiting for him to let us out of that tiny opening in the pentagon through which we must
exit our caves, break free of an ouroboros locking us up in a flawed intergalactic
realm, an escape that underscores the essence of existence, pivots our notion that essence yes
precedes existence as opposed to the view of existentialists such as Sartre, that the reverse
is the case, albeit specifying that assertion to humans, predicating it on the
notion that we are free to choose hence determine who we become: freedom to choose we also hold.

Yes, folks we affirm the notion of freedom to choose but situate that freedom within a snake,
within constraints that are not only social, cultural, economic, political, or yea
whatever else physically operational in a voided space, but also within those
operational outside the physical aspect of the continuum of consciousness dear
mates, in its immaterial aspect that engenders the physical aspect, in other words,
the essence of the existent physicality we term our reality yea, and essence
that is transcendental in some important respect termed noumena, the primal source in a void
outside a void, the flickering flame in all of us the metamorphic cord that transmutations
herein of anamorphic states may engender as we seek to break free of the chains of deadly
snakes, of anacondas doing their darnedest to lead us along the path of death in void O yea.

Folks, treading the path of death doing evil in the world only serves us well that we may yea be
interned forever in a flawed situation to sustain a snake, to be fodder for the beast
for aye for rice, folks for a bowl of rice, that's it! Should that be more important to us than our souls
dear mates? As quixotic as this question may sound who really thinks we are chasing shadows trying
to solve an insolvable riddle, that we should throw our hands up in the air O yes and become
aporetic rather than turn aporia into an opportunity to peep into
the other, so-called un-understandable side perhaps serendipity may give us a smile?
Who does that is herein in an intergalactic jail? Maybe some of us cannot come to terms
with the fact that we are all slaves: maybe it's the stage-managed money or privilege, you know, the
perceived racial superiority, even intra-white or intra-black they have that becloud.

Yes, folks, maybe something is beclouding their mental states, who knows? Let's face it folks we are herein
enslaved to sustain a snake, to keep a beast 'alive,' never mind our metaphors, but to what end?
These are questions we cannot afford to toss let's digest deeper into the materiality-
immateriality conundrum in a voided space to try to better comprehend yea
goings on in our world, what is going on in our lives, and in the lives of ghosts, the beings herein
humans and 'humans' yea, the crux of the matter of matters that do not exist but that do yea
exist, along a continuum of consciousness dear mates, interacting yea in glowing school
buses in the woods and on city streets, a continuum of consciousness we hope to better
figure for the good of all, that we may look forward to our transmutations yea, without a doubt
to metamorphic be from anamorphic states, a more perfect union embrace in a void.

Our explorations of the interactiveness of the constituents of amalgams will yes,
hopefully, buttress our notion of consciousness and how it operates herein, that it is the
manifestation of the energy exchanges between entities that are themselves outcomes
in here yes of wavefunction collapses that reflect O yea an unspecified variable
the interpretation of which the Copenhagen interpretation concerns herein O yes,
the requirement of a consciousness to observe its measurement to situate it dear folks is
a metaphysical 'interpretation' some contest, arguing that the termination of
the motion of a subatomic particle ends its dynamic mien, which is essentially
its static mien, an argument that coincides with our notion of the interactiveness of
materiality and immateriality on a continuum of consciousness!

It is an argument that may explain the appearance of phantoms as us and us as phantoms
yea in a voided space, the interactiveness and interchangeability of dynamic
and static mien instructive regarding who or what is 'seeing' or 'thinking' we refer to yes
holding tight to our views on matters that do not exist and exist in dichotomous ways, you
know as empiricists or rationalists for example, considering consciousness in the
sense of the 'awareness' of an individual's personal identity and O yes in
relation to the world, jaw-jawing herein on whether the brain is its seat or simply that of
cognition and perception for example, an approach to consciousness that misses the point folks
about what some traditions refer to as 'possession by spirits' that must be exorcised yes,
others, as 'multiple personalities or dissociative identity disorder.'

Indeed, yet others refer to this other approach to consciousness recognizing 'amalgams'
as the unified entity that consciousness is, an entity that manifests herein in
our reality the prevailing consciousness among the various consciousnesses that are
its constituents, all exerting relative measures of influence on the outcomes of their
interactions in energy transactions as we postulate. These terms suggest experiences
we may interpret as inconsistent with the notion of an individual consciousness,
the 'awareness' yea by someone of their 'personal identity,' when historicism for
instance says hidden processes we also call entities over which we lack control tweak us
and our world dear mates, figuring out who or what these entities or demons or processes are
that control us but that we cannot control a task we must accomplish in a voided space, yes.

So, folks, we cannot and must not dismiss the possibility of aliens being present in
our midst, entities that have been here since immemorial days setting things up herein, you know,

the politico-socio-cultural institutions of societal balkanization
and division, the veritable means of control that are so entrenched in void today even
legislators struggle to change, just think about the our laws, of yore and now; why folks are things so
complicated even legislators find its language easy to 'manipulate' to deny
women control over their own body even threaten to throw them in jail if they asserted
those rights, why folks? Should we, therefore, not be curious to know O yes who or what these behind-the-
scene entities or processes that continue to tweak our world perhaps through their surrogates we
are more used to than the walking sticks, something that reveals our true status as nothing but slaves, yea?

We should! No one knows better than a thief to spot their footprints on a rock than other thief! So, we
the ghosts know best how to catch other ghosts: but we must first admit we are also ghosts herein in
a void, we must see ourselves as materialized immateriality in a voided space,
we must first imagine these so-called aliens mingling in our world as being us, perhaps a mates
a neighbour, or a friend, in whom a prevalent consciousness manifests herein as the so-called
'personal identity' yes, the so-called 'personality' yea, the so-called unified whole
that is nothing but the sum of its parts, its parts with uneven energy endowments, money
for instance, that heads befuddle to varying degrees creating the enabling milieu for
perpetuating the entrenched notion of the 'human condition,' the global poverty here.

Book 6

Yes, folks, whether we know it or not we all dwell, in our formulation, in poverty here so
pervasive its potential negative impact on us all, individually and O yes
collectively cannot be gainsaid, and to think that some entities are behind our woes, you know,
that some cryptic lunatic entity or entities mystify us with such impunity
is truly hard to fathom, even as phantoms! Some herein may hex poetic license for our
quixotism, others, some sort of 'softness of our brains,' or whatever, unable perhaps they
are to fathom phantoms yes! Indeed, some may consider us heretics unable they may be
yes to yoke angels and ghosts, you know, aliens, forgetting that anyone may be baptized as
a faith leader once said, embodying the spirit of inclusiveness we talk about yes to
foster peace and harmony in our world, after all we could have wished our visitors away, yes.

We would have been able to wish them away all these years if we really could, wouldn't we? That they
are still here, therefore, indicates we probably couldn't! O well, we think they were and are still here,
those ghosts, because we are here, the ghosts, the matters we think do not exist but also exist yes, our
notion of existence consistent herein folks with our notion of the materiality-
immateriality continuum, yet, we must bear in mind we 'situate' dear folks the
operations of this continuum in a block universe we postulate yes an inter-
dimensional realm or its constituents begets, implicitly, engendering a spacetime
continuum, an inter-dimensional realm begetting an intergalactic realm O yes,
restricting our consideration for now to our universe wherein the stars dance around us
pre-Copernican style, what we dare to say in our formulation, in our poetic fiction.

Yes, folks, we dare to say stars are here imitating life, reality put differently folks,
materialized essence or phenomena, so folks, we need to 'suspend' an anamorphic
zeitgeist, one in which an accretion of millennia of knowledge guide our thoughts to embrace yes
a paradigmatic shift, Kuhnian style, wherein grand narratives of yore either melt away or
take the back seat for novel ideas, no matter how quixotic or incompatible with
dated ones, that novel ones may flourish, that we are not declared heretics for exploring the
skies with a LUCIFER aka LBT Near Infrared Spectroscopic Utility
with Camera and Integral Field Unit for Extragalactic Research instrument yes, the
LBT, Large Binocular Telescope, perhaps looking for, guess what, aliens? It's now called
the LUCI telescope by the way: what's in a name! There could be a lot folks, much more than we think.

So, what are we waiting for? We have instruments and we reason, we have the will and we are still
alive, let's go folks let's fly away venture into the intergalactic realm yes to tryst with
angels dine with ghosts O yea, with our kin in skies above low low! Perhaps we will meet kindred spirits that
may sing with us dance to our serenades, maybe we'll chorus out there the music of the spheres with
heavenly nightingales, piculets drumming away in style ravens garbed in twinkling trench coats hid
behind their designer 'bones,' just like the women and men in black hide their eyes in our precious world,
let's go folks let's elucidate our world, ferret the cryptic entities lurking behind our eyes
tell them all we can see them that this time they are the ones in their 'darkness' that has turned yea against
them so much the table has turned in our favour yea: now we can see them but they cannot see us,
the people are now in charge of their lives and are no longer going to be anybody's slaves.

'No more slaves,' we will shout atop the mountain to the heavens up above and to the world yes of
Hades down below. We will enjoin all in the realms to celebrate our freedom in a voided
space with us all yea, material and otherwise dear mates in the intergalactic realm yes
wherein we dwell, a world of ghosts and 'ghosts,' where everyone dear folks in amalgams abides O yea,
yes we will all in peace and harmony rejoice we're free at last to choices make whereof our goal
clear in our minds prepared for changes we anticipate living a virtuous life herein in
a void, why we will celebrate, for we would have escaped from fangs of deadly snakes, from the belly
of an ouroboros belly of the beast the Leviathan keeping us all enslaved here in
Platonic caves where shadows we all chase, no matter knight or knave, until we break the chains, yes the
manacles that have us bonded to bowls of rice we trade in for our souls confused by ghosts O yes.

Yes, bemused by razzmatazz in awe of spectral states, intimidated herein by 'glowing' yea
amorphousness, puzzled by materiality immateriality begets, in awe
of us, ourselves, dear mates and understandably so, yes for it must be hard to swallow this weird
notion of aliens being here in our midst no matter how famished we are, you know folks, to be
uncertain some triple-headed erectile reptile is not what is standing in queue behind us
looking like us whose spit is poison at its 'best,' or is able to wallop humans whole yes not
even with anything to wash down their meal, dear mates! That is hard to ponder on the way to do
errands or on the train to work! Yet, we must not be in denial dismiss these matters that we
think do not exist but think do, betwixt perhaps because we think we are spirit beings, that we do
not physically exist as spirits but we do as beings, the humans we are we see we feel.

Yes, we believe we exist as humans, each of us as a physical entity that's born and
that dies, which implies the 'naturalness' of our 'quixotic' formulations folks, O yes, which some
empiricists herein seem to loathe, the contradiction inherent in which the prejudice yes,
manifest in their discriminations against others, based on race, religion, sex and yes skin
colour for example, reveals, you know, ghosts loathing the notion of physical ghosts, or folks put
differently, ghosts loathing themselves, a notion we will keep harping upon to stress its very
pivotal role in our basic formulation of the mechanics of our world, one that will shear
the Russian doll that hides our so-called controllers here in plain sight yea, a notion that they also
seem folks to detest, apparently preferring to hide their eyes under their designer 'bones,' their
funny eyes conceal under a hood, their vector-legs hide in a trench coat: but we all now see them.

We see them alright, we see them with our very eyes, the eyes of the alliances yea in the
amalgams we formed that are prevalent in our manifest consciousness dear mates, why we see this
phenomenon called consciousness differently than the zeitgeist does, which is hardly surprising
given the paradigmatic shift in mindsets that our formulation entails, and much more, yet,
folks we cannot run away from the reality we share, the realization at last that
aliens live among us, one that raises fundamental questions regarding who or what we
are and whereof reality is, so, folks, are we going to continue to hide herein in
denial until a popping pumpkin shows up in our garden saying 'hello?' Or are we all
going to be prepared to say 'hello' back? The choice is ours, folks. We need to be ready to take
important decisions regarding our lives and our void, decisions that reflect on us.

Decisions that show a deep comprehension of our void and the existential and issues
we all face dear mates, including our so-called bosses that must be fully aware O yes of the

differential energy endowments of walking sticks and popping pumpkins for example,
and of the potential of many other stars planning to come dancing around us here in our
very precious void, so folks, these are not joking matters yea, these are survival matters that may
see us all being wolfed en-masse by some 'amalgams' of letters and numbers that cannot even yea
survive for too long outside a host! Lord have mercy! Let's get serious mates and confront folks the
issues we face yea with the strength of togetherness and dignity. We owe it to our children
and our grandchildren and to all those coming after us to leave a legacy they will be proud
to build upon, not a legacy of shame, not one of corruption, bigotry, and ineptitude, yea.

Let us not leave a legacy of hatred folks, we ought to keep working hard folks to make our world
a better place for all of us ghosts, mattered or not, after all, we all abide right here in our
precious world, our precious consciousness that manifests all consciousnesses yea, we have no other
place to dwell in no place to call our own but here in the consciousness we build as the arrow of
time marches on relentlessly and we hope to find that goldilocks moment to harness O yes
entropic energy for positive gain, to build a better world for everyone of us in
a dying void, not accelerate its demise caring not about the delicate balance of
the ecosystem in which we survive and thrive dear mates: we need to care about climate change folks, we
need to care about saving our world, and by the extension, ourselves and, frankly folks we have no
time to waste, we must not procrastinate, we must forge ahead and elucidate our world, O yes.

Book 7

Let's do it, folks, let us unveil the mysteries of void, let us endeavour yea to better know
ourselves that we may better know our world, that we may not continue to be slaves in a void not
knowing who or what is in control in void, or how they operate yea to lord it over us,
only realizing that they do and we seem able not to resist their hegemonic ways,
flustered by which we succumb to 'learned helplessness' simply get on with our lives, or whatever is
left of it afraid to lose the bowl of rice on which we so rely to stay alive in void, O
what a sorry state, one we must all try to change we reckon or endure for aye, which underscores
the point about making choices folks we cannot wish away, one that no amount of dodging will
ever leave alone a mind tormented our miserableness ever with us in a void, yea
ahead of us forever herein unless we make that change, break free of serfdom dear mates, O yes.

Think deep about it, folks, think about the huge difference herein between an anamorphic and
a metamorphic existence in a mattered state an inter-dimensional realm begets yes
even in our intergalactic realm, think about even just the joy of knowing where we head on
our pilgrimage in this arena of trials and tribulations no matter who or what we
are, after all we all must die, indisposed afore or not, we all must exit this space whether
we like it or not, whether we are walking sticks manifest or a triple-headed beast, yes no
matter how much we like to make peace or prefer to make war, to gang up against one another
for spite or whatever yea, to destroy one another's career to advance our own, no matter
how many times we pray per day or never pray at all: we will all die in the end dear mates. So,
do we choose to free ourselves from slavery or live our lives as slaves? The choice is ours, folks, it is.

It surely is our prerogative to exist in whatever form, be it as serfs, or as free
or shackled ghosts, we must choose the path we want to tread herein in a void: we must all choose
between a path of life and a path of death, we must all decide whether or not we want to sell
our soul folks for a bowl of rice drown in a razzmatazz we must all leave behind when we exit
the void, or prepare to enter Eden's gate our transmutation starting even here in our void,
it is that simple folks: take the rice or free the soul. Just to be sure, we are not talking here folks
about some grain, we are talking about whether or not we want to worship Satan, as yea some
traditions refer to evil manifest, you know, doing evil deeds herein in our void,
you know, sell our soul to the devil, or we want to live virtuously doing good deeds herein
folks, that is what we are talking about, nothing more, that is the choice we must make folks, and fast, yes.

So, the struggle continues, for it is a struggle to escape the beast, but we remember yes
Frederick Douglass who once said 'if there is no struggle there is no progress,' the struggle herein
continues folks, the struggle to free ourselves from the bondage whoever or whatever in here
controlling our void has us in, we must not falter folks and we must triumph, and we will working
together to improve our world, this is our goal folks this is our song, our spectral serenades, our
songs of hope here to succeed dear mates. Success is the ultimate objective we so bear in mind
realizing it is one thing to speculate on what is going on in our void and yea quite
another to break free of the slavery and oppression we experience in our daily
lives, at home at school at work wherever folks we all are engaged, experiences some people want
us to believe is a so-called human condition, a condition of poverty folks, O yes.

It is a condition of poverty not just of the material but also, and folks more
importantly, of the spiritual, into which this conditioning into believing we
are here to suffer plunges us dear mates, whereas we are not here to suffer, we are all here to
enjoy the bounties of nature and leave a better world for those coming after us to also
enjoy, we are here to prove our worth and improve our lot as we prepare for our next journey on
our pilgrimage, as some traditions may term our peregrinations herein in a voided space,
in an intergalactic realm, which is why we must take the issue of making the right choices
seriously folks, regardless of our view on matters that do not exist and we think exist,
after all it the our actions not our forms that count, a triple-headed entity is not yea
necessarily malevolent and a single-headed entity like us, may be, O yes.

So, folks we must reject poverty, we must not at all allow this bogus notion pumped into
our heads of the human condition to hold sway in our minds, it is a ploy to intimidate
us and keep us all enslaved, to demoralize us into thinking we are all doomed and must all
thankfully take the crumbs thrown at us dear mates: there is nothing farther than the truth, we are not dumb
nor are we doomed, except maybe in the retarded minds of those persons that have reasons to dumb
us down, to enslave and control us, persons to whom we must declare we have had enough of their
nonsense and that no matter how much they pretend to be tone-deaf we are forging ahead setting
ourselves free of their hegemony in our precious world, that is what we need to do dear mates, what
we need to tell ourselves we can do and must do O yea, folks we cannot afford to pass up this
chance to free ourselves choose the path of life ascension yes in sight, our goal attainable dear mates.

We know some folks may think we are nonsensical: we are not at all surprised and folks, we will not
be surprised to sound even worse to others that may not agree O yes with our formulation
of consciousness and, in effect, with our notion yea of amalgams being who we really are, yes:
everyone is entitled to their views and no one should have to feel pressured to agree with our
persuasions yea, albeit we hope that we can all still join hands to make our world a better
place for everyone of us, the key issue we are trying to get across to everyone in
void, one which we hold forces operating behind the scenes appear to want to be sure we do
yea not achieve, at least not to benefit us and make us harder to control, this is the crux
of the matter folks, to keep us perpetually enslaved, to find out why we have ventured yea
into eclectic knowledge sources including quantum physics, mathematics, and history.

Yes, and into religious studies among the many others our eyes now wide open and our
vision sharper more focused O yes, more so that our hidden bosses don't even seem to know that
we can now see them, they appear not to see us seeing them dear mates, or maybe they are simply
pretending who knows? It does not matter whether or not they are pretending, what matters is that
we are not, we are serious and focused on our goals, so folks let us put what we have learned yea
into practice work to save ourselves and to save our world, let us continue to try answering
the questions some persons think are impossible to ask and should not have been asked to begin with
folks, questions regarding the reasons our bosses want to keep us enslaved for example O yea,
the reasons folks why it appears our controllers want to keep us in poverty, material
and spiritual, and why they are hiding if they had nothing to hide: we'll seek the answers yea.

Indeed, we will. We have come to the conclusion that we have controllers and that they operate
both materially and immaterially yes, which is why we talk about matters that

do not exist that we think exist, why we talk about a continuum of consciousness here
along which we all must interchangeably exist, and it does not appear we are the only
ones that are quixotic since some of our leaders, alive or dead, have warned us about the presence
of aliens in our midst, not to mention the many reports by our folks of sightings herein
of unidentified flying objects and alien abductions and recent interests of
governments in investigating what is termed unidentified aerial phenomena:
earlier sources also support the presence of these alien visitors herein,
including the Anunnaki, 'sky people' said to have genetically engineered us.

'We wrestle not against flesh and blood, but against principalities, against powers, against the
rulers of the darkness of this world, against a spiritual wickedness in high places,' yea.
Paul could not have said this in vain in his letter to the Ephesians O yes, yet, and despite all
these supporting evidences we still doubt the notion of immateriality yes on
a continuum with materiality, at least some physicists do, not to mention folks
that have nothing to do with physics, yes, many of us simply don't buy the idea yes that
anyone other than God or some deity, of which many exists in different cultures
and traditions, for instance, made or engineered us, that is even if they believed in the
notion of creation rather than in evolution, or in fact in nothing at all as our
origin dear mates: we hold on to our formulation and continue to work to save our world.

Book 8

Yes, mates. We will keep working toward our goal as hard as we can, we recognize there will be no easy way out of our quagmire but know there will be a way out, we know there are likely many more people that believe in similar ideas as ours than people that do not and, working together and persuading others to join us we will find a way out. So, folks we are not alone, most cultures worldwide believe in what is generally termed the supernatural, they believe in entities that exist in otherworldly realms, be they Satan, demons and fairies, mammywater or in flying saucers, flying palaces and in vinamas, they believe in sky people, reptilian people or in ant people, so, we are not alone in talking about ghosts and immaterial entities O yes, it is important to mention this yea to underline the fact that such widespread beliefs in similar ideas, including in God, count.

They attest to the reasonableness of our notion of what consciousness is and how it here operates collectively yes rather than individually dear mates, its seemingly yea personal nature actually a manifestation of the outcomes here of energy exchanges and alliances among consciousnesses comprising our amalgams dear mates. We realize our notion of consciousness may be dismissed by some people, after all, dear mates the Trinitarian doctrine continues to be controversial even among adherents to the same underlying faith! The point here is that our notion of us being amalgams is not new, yet it tends to be more convenient, apparently, for us to ignore anything to do with ghosts, perhaps it is too scary to mull, perhaps it conflicts with our doctrinal views, maybe it is inconsistent with our scientific views or it is not politically correct.

So, folks we ignore what is not expedient, right? We dismiss the presence of aliens in our midst because we don't want to entertain such scary notions or breach our core religious or ideological beliefs, or because we do not want to hurt our spouse or our friend O yea, or a deeply spiritual person close to us, yes, spiritual, right? You see folks, we do these things seemingly oblivious to their implications for ourselves and for our world, O yes including our continuing enslavement and the prospects of our precious void becoming yea extinct! Let's dig a little deeper into these consequences dear mates. By not acknowledging the presence of aliens in our midst we are missing a golden opportunity to free ourselves from the yoke of slavery yes, we are showing a lack of understanding of who or what we really may be and of the mechanics of what our void, our consciousness, really is, yes.

O yes, folks we are ignoring what our reality is and how it operates, in effect, denying ourselves a chance to figure the nuances of the metaphors we have been using here to describe our world in relation to the goings on in void that create the sense of being enslaved, a serfdom from which we want to escape, so, folks, we miss knowing that we are really yea trying to escape from ourselves that prevalent consciousnesses in our amalgams have managed to trap in servitude which, in relation to our void becoming extinct implies the actions of these prevalent consciousnesses annihilating us, let's say, the weaker, defeated dumbed down consciousnesses that will therefore no longer manifest an material 'reality' or void, as we 'knew,' it, witness the weirdness going on now in void: the new 'reality' will comprise that of whatever consciousnesses the prevalent consciousnesses have granted the 'right,' to exist, yea.

The new world will be made up of legislators that are proficient at and willing to create
and pass voter suppression laws for example and a zombified populace waiting for their
turns to be thrown a bowl of rice and to be later wolfed! You see, folks why we all need to take these
issues seriously just in case matters really panned out this way? It is unlikely yea that
anyone would want to ignore consciousnesses in our midst that manifest such demonic plans
for the human race, yet their actions follow them around and speak for them their intent hidden in
plain sight or who or what else would want to make laws that jail women for affirming control over
their bodies or promulgate laws that further worsen yes climate change and jeopardize dear mates the
delicate ecosystem of our voided space, who folks, who? We will have to face the facts of our lives at some
point folks, hopefully, before it's too late. We can change our fate, after all we are the ghosts, O yes.

There may be varied schools of thought regarding the mechanics of our world, ranging dear mates from the
conventional school that sees us as individual entities or personalities with
our individual consciousnesses created or evolved acting in a perceptible
world, to those seeing us as amalgams of consciousnesses manifest in a void, to yet folks
others seeing us as illusory, non-existent states. We have the choice to believe in none,
any or all of these formulations none of which can claim epistemological truth, all
of which are speculative folks in so far as none of us can prove our position. Regardless,
the truth must lie somewhere we may eventually reach, somewhere we hold O yes is a state of
perfection we place in a hypothetical 'place' we refer to as Eden yea, a place of
eternal light that never dims, where we all hope to be to yoke with ane, the primal source dear mates.

Yes, the primal source whereof we do not and may never know in our present anamorphic state,
why we seek ascension to be metamorphic yea, so, folks, this is our own believe, the believe
we are here to have a chance to actualize living a virtuous life treading the path of
goodness not that of evil yea, creating opportunities for everyone to express their
rights to vote for whoever their conscience picks, not pass legislations that will suppress their rights so
to do, so folks, you see where we are coming from and where we are going yea, democracy is
'ordained' as the way for us to organize human society and affairs: we all know what
happened to the ancient Greeks with their conquest by the Spartans heralding the demise yes of their
democracy, which should remind us that democracy has enemies not just outside but yes
within its borders yea, both equally deadly foes we must never allow to have their way, yes.

We must never allow any ghost to destroy our democracy folks, we must never let them
render us all extinct, we must affirm our fundamental human right to freely express our
choices at the ballot box, and we must all go out to vote come rain or whatever yea, we must
be at polls to cast our votes no matter what the enemies of democracy do we must tell
them they will fail. We must employ peaceful methods and never resort to violence to affirm
our rights, for we will be falling into their trap doing that, we must not let them fool us into
believing in some lousy notion of 'insurrection' and we must not be fooled into thinking
that 'balkanization' will free us from slavery and oppression, on the other hand, it will
only make us easier targets to control and wolf, O yes, with the application of the
'Policy of Encirclement' for example. There is strength in numbers folks, doubtless, yes, dear mates.

There is, indeed. Witness how we were able to kick out some so-called 'boss' at the polls yea not long
ago, some ex-this ex-that now making noise in their rabbit hole still as deluded as ever

they won an election in which they were roundly trounced: who cares about a deluded fiend? We are
moving on folks. They may choose to rot in their rabbit holes crying and moaning about their spilled milk
for aye, we are forging ahead turning lead into gold, yes folks, we are making our world a much
better, happier place for everyone of us, notwithstanding walking sticks and yes triple-
headed snakes, entities masquerading here thinking we cannot and do not see their ears! What? Let
it out folks, we see the flickering eyes and ears and more: it's disclosure time we've had enough of
nonsense going on in void. They may think everyone is dead but we will show them at the polls that
we are all alive and well, that they may need higher doses of chlorpromazine to fix their pates.

Yes, folks, enough is enough! Can't folks even make a dime anymore? Does someone always have
to change the rules to help the so-called rich maintain their grip on wealth herein and prevent the so-called
poor, by the way regardless of colour, race, or creed, foraying into the goldmines of the rich?
Lord have mercy! Open your eyes folks, what happens to the more than five hundred herein that will now
face charges for an insurrection? Thrown under the boss? Of course, all those that encouraged them and
goaded them are walking free while our poor folks lose all the little they've got and languish in jail! What in
the realms can be more unfair a so-called leader can do to these folks? To add insult yes to
injury, this leader boastfully claims they have a grip on the folks they have misled and that now face
the prospects of spending many years in jail separated from their families and loved ones yes
unable to send their children to school and to cater for their families yes: poor things; so sad!

Book 9

We all ought to empathize with our folks and take this issue of entities controlling us all surreptitiously very seriously dear mates, we ought to take this matter of matters we think do not exist but think exist very, very seriously O yes. We must not at all disregard those flickering ears and eyes and must not kid ourselves thinking they are illusions, or even hallucinations, you know, that we need a dose or two of chlorpromazine, rather folks, we must concede God, or whatever we call who we believe deserves the status of a deity, is showing us what we seek and ought to see, perhaps to drive home the fact that there are aliens right here in our midst, alien amalgams parasitizing ours, a benevolent act that underscores our point O yes regarding communication between the block universe dear folks, a universal amalgamation and an inter-dimensional realm we cannot explain.

We may not be able to explain it but we can extrapolate it to that between matters we do not think exist and think exist, what we term a continuum of consciousness that may or may not manifest in the reality we share, in other words, this communication between an intergalactic and an inter-dimensional realm indicates we may not be that quixotic after all talking about ghosts aping ghosts, assuming seeing those flickering ears and eyes are, indeed, acts of God, and sharing concerns dear mates about a supposedly yes entropically moribund world, right? We may be on the right track talking about parasites and bugs and viruses and prions and flickering eyes and ears menacing us all herein in our space, invading us with their demonic venoms softening our hippocampus and prefrontal cortex Turing us into 'happy' retards creating chaos in the very consciousness we share we call void.

Yes folks, what we call reality, these entities corrupting this consciousness manifest in the accretions of a block universe that an inter-dimensional realm begets, in other words slowly rendering us herein extinct, our world, that is and all there is in it, yes, everything our consciousness manifests, which means what the emergent by consciousness manifests as reality yes dear mates which, as such, predicates on the consciousness and the changes it undergoes, good or bad, all sorts of constituents of amalgams bring upon it, why we must be concerned about malevolent entities tweaking our void trying to destroy us all: we have no time to waste folks as these adverse changes to our consciousness evident herein in our constantly changing reality signal potentially ominous developments in our precious world, the end of our democracy and the beginning of fascism for instance yes.

As incredible as our formulations may sound to some folks we must not dismiss dear folks the possibility, if not even, the probability of there being aliens in our midst, no folks we must not, we must not toss the notion of the enemy within, our void invaded by viruses, bugs and sundry fiends that are, for all intents and purposes, us: we must not at all folks ignore the idea that we are our worst foes herein, whether we know it or not, an idea consistent with our belief in us all here in a voided all being material ghosts of immaterial ghosts, as such, responsible in some way, through the alliances we forge, and the decisions those alliances make at all levels, individual and O yes collectively as groups, religious or political or any other group, for goings on in our voided space, which underscores the point about each one of taking charge of our lives, yes.

It highlights the need for everyone to control their decision-making, not allow ourselves to
be zombified blindly following a so-called leader into their rabbit hole. We need to be strong for ourselves
that some predator-leader does not see us as emotionally needy and easily manipulated, or even at all,
manipulable, yes, for it is such perceptions that fires intimidation, threats of withdrawal of the emotional and
social or financial or whatever support we created the impression we so badly need from the group, sadly a
threat that is often effective in securing our capitulation and compliance to 'group think,' a wicked,
Machiavellian tactic that traps us in these so-called groups that are more aptly cults, yes, they
are cults, personality cults that these days make their predecessors such as the 'Jonestown' and the
so-called 'revolutionary suicide' of 1978 in which more than 900 persons died yes
poisoned by cyanide their leader ordered them to take, look benign, a whole nation at risk, yes!

Dear mates, that we live in an age in which democracy is being viciously and shamelessly
attacked with the support, tacitly and otherwise of leaders of faith and other groups in whom
our folks repose their trust to shepherd them on the pilgrimage in faith cannot be gainsaid. This is
nothing but a betrayal of trust, not to mention that folks know where to go for political
guidance; they know they could get that by joining a political party! So, folks we need to call
out these traitors parleying with brandishers of Holy Scriptures for political gain, we need
to tell them we see them in technicolor and know about the dirty games they play, we need to
let them know we are no fools and are longer taking orders from them, that we will follow our minds
with immediate effect O yes. These traitors remind us of the varieties O yes of
consciousnesses lurking in our midst some clad in white, perhaps even purple soutanes herein, yes.

So, folks we must be vigilant and stop showing reverence for crooks, more importantly, we must
stop taking their lousy orders stop attacking democracy yes, worse still on behalf of some
retarded cult leader feeling strong spoiling for a fight, we must be strong for ourselves and decide,
not to fight anyone but to tread the path of life, join hands with others to work together for
the good of all. We must no longer let anyone exploit our faith we not allow others to
take us for a ride messing with our heads pumping lies, big and small, into our minds via tweets and yes
messages on social media, blogs, podcasts and other mass news outlets, we must not allow
ourselves to become social media slaves; not even nations should let social media yea
dictate government policies albeit not dismissing opinions expressed through yes this
medium, one so awash in misinformation vigilance becomes necessary O yes.

Indeed, folks. It becomes absolutely necessary to separate wheat from chaff, as the old
saying goes. So, it is important that we take decisions, at personal and at collective
levels, for our own good and folks, for the good of all, to save ourselves and our precious world, and folks
we have no time to waste, for we know we are not here forever folks, and we do not know when we'll
be gone, we do not know for how much longer we will be here in a voided space, why we must act
and not procrastinate, yes we must act take decisions on our own not wait for anyone, not
a group member, a leader, colleagues or anyone, to 'advise' on whether to tread the path of
life or the path of death, we should decide on our own to do good or to evil do, after all
we will face our fate all alone dear mates, we will be there alone on judgement day to head yes for
heaven or to head for hell as some traditions hold, we will be there on own all alone dear mates.

We must realize we can moan all day all night herein folks about slavery, prejudice, about

discrimination, injustice, about whatever wrong humans are visiting upon one
another, and we may agitate as much as we can but we must ask ourselves why these issues
persist, why they seem to have been with us for millennia and seem to not want to go away
despite the efforts we have made in the past, including going to war to set things straight we must
ask ourselves why these issues are still here in one form or another yes: what is going on? Really
folks, what is happening in our precious void, or shall we say, yes in our collective consciousness
manifest in the reality we share? We can almost be certain folks has answered yea this
question in various ways through the ages, some similarly to ours, so, we are not claiming
to have the correct answer folks but we have formulations we continue to explore herein.

Yes, we continue to explore our formulations as working hypotheses to figure out
our world: we really want to comprehend our world, we want to make the world a better place for all,
for everyone of us, to achieve which goal we need to take decisions that will serve not only
our interests but also the common good, which requires us understanding and overcoming
obstacles in our way, seen or unseen, material or immaterial yes, why we have
been stressing the need to not rule out the presence of malevolent entities here in our midst
manipulating void, or collective consciousness O yea, which places the onus on all of
us to come together join hands to save ourselves and save our precious void, a task folks we all must
accomplish one folks we must not delay, not with a virus in our face threatening to claim our
fate, to render us all extinct, folks much herein yea is at stake, we have no time to waste, O yes.

Book 10

We must not be aporetic because the issues we face seem enduring mates, it may just be disclosure time we see yes what we see, in any case the struggle must continue we must play our part in emancipating void, our collective consciousness lift herein in a void, we may just be the ones to make the change, our consciousness may just have reached an inflection point ready to change direction yes, who knows? Here we are though talking about breaking free yes of the shackles of slavery herein in a void: we're working on it, determined to free ourselves folks from the fangs of snakes! So, we are following in the footsteps of our predecessors and we are not giving up on ourselves not giving up on our world, exploring our issues from eclectic viewpoints to which we are accustomed or not, our belief and faith in our fellow humans unshaken yea, our ability to come together to overcome obstacles in our we, dear mates, relish yes.

Times are, doubtless, changing mates we are forging ahead unfazed. We are all looking at a brighter future for ourselves, our children and grandchildren and for all of us, a future herein free of interference with our rights to vote unforced or hampered yea in any way, one we can all here applaud and be proud of dear mates, and we are prepared to work hard to attain this noble goal free ourselves from pain, escape the tarantulas yea, afraid no more to seek to know the secrets void secretes, our fate declare is now yea in our minds so mote it be dear mates. There is no doubt it has taken us a long time to get to where we are: it really has been a long journey to a point we can face our foes and tell them we can see and hear them and we are no more scared to think and to decide on our own without any help from any intermediary or anyone at all: we are no longer intimidated by anyone's threats, we are forging full blast ahead.

We are blazing the trail we love, folks digging deep into the world of elves using whatever gen we are able to find scavenging eclectic sources yes, no longer are we afraid yes to ignore the 'don't ask don't explain just calculate' doctrine that some physicists may have come across, our mantra being 'seek and ye shall find,' and yes, we seek and hope to find more information herein regarding ghosts, that is regarding us, more so, regarding the ability yes of certain consciousnesses to hold sway in our voided space, able to control us and our world, we want to know who or what 'inhabits' us doing this tweaking messing with our pates for so very long, and does not seem to have any plans to leave us alone and stop menacing us, something that has us wondering if this thing could not indeed be us, to the extent that our formulation sees us as amalgams O yea, composed of consciousnesses engaged in energy interactions yes.

So folks, we are thinking that one or more alliances of consciousnesses become prevalent at any point in time and perhaps for aye, representing goodness or evil for example manifest in void. As such, we may conceive of evil as sundry consciousnesses O yes with similar goals forming a consciousness of evil that is actualized, or better still folks, materialized in void. In other words the ghosts in this alliance may be walking sticks, vectors and popping pumpkins yes, other forms forming alliances and manifesting goodness in void, which means that an exorcist may be trying to rid the possessed of a monstrous viper or yes a massive spider yes, which suggests not only that we may indeed be amalgams but also that we may overcome the forces of darkness that have somehow managed to inhabit us, you know, those smelly entities! The point here is that we are all ghosts comprising accretions of ghosts.

Yes, accretions of all sorts of forms lurking herein in void dear mates over an atavistic
epigenetic epiphenomena that is the amalgam we are, why we have yea been
emphasizing the functions of these entities rather than their forms: it is their actions and how
they affect us that must concern us as this is what determines whether we are considered slaves
or whatever yea, it is what may underlie the gumption of legislators to propose bills
to send women to jail for affirming their rights to control their bodies or yes to pass laws to
suppress the rights of our folks to vote, after all, we are saying these malevolent entities
inhabit us, that they are constituent consciousnesses in the amalgam that each
of us is yea, so, we are saying in effect that we are these ghosts externalized, the prevalent or dominant
consciousness able to express itself unhindered through us in our thoughts and actions: scary eh?

It is indeed a scary state to even contemplate and may explain why the issues we face
have been with us folks since immemorial days and appear to have no intentions of ever
going away, right? Right. We are the ghosts tweaking the ghosts folks, after all we are all children of
the stars as some traditions hold, and we have been waging internecine intergalactic wars
for a long time yea, so we have been establishing hegemonies over one another that
changing intergalactic alliances shift, which may explain yes historical events and
epochs that we are not suggesting are not value-laden folks, you know, that may not twist events
to suit the winners of the wars we wage, you know, to claim Julius Caesar ordered herein folks the
immolation of the Library of Alexandria determined to catch Ptolemy O yes,
perhaps in its ruins! By the way our use of 'herein' is deliberate, it means actions by 'ghosts.'

It implies the actions in question were initiated by ghosts in the immaterial
realm to be decoded and materialized in our void, to emphasize the operations
of the continuum of consciousness in the mechanics of our void and, perhaps dear folks more
importantly to stress how we as the ghosts in the immaterial realm are responsible
for goings on in the material realm, in our world, which underscores the need for us all to
figure the nuances of the experiences we have in our sojourn through life yea, the so-called
human condition and what we need to do to improve our lives and to make the world a better
place for everyone of us, so, folks, we must admit we may be missing the point not properly
conceptualizing consciousness dear mates, we may be missing a golden opportunity
here to achieve our aim of breaking free of snakes taking a literal view of vipers O yes.

We may be missing the point misunderstanding the metaphors and euphemisms we use to
drive home the points we make and label us quixotic nuts, even demons that need to have herein
a psychological 'assessment,' but hey, what is in a name? By admitting we may need to
make some adjustments to our mindsets and be more accommodating of divergent views we may
be getting closer to finally figuring who or what we are and why we may be able
to rid ourselves of our flawed atavistic traits, a more desirable outcome it seems than yea
calling one another names and punishing folks for holding a different view than ours, herein
strapping folks to the wheel, albeit a new-medieval version of the contraption yea, even
beheading them, literally and figuratively yes, you know, attitudinal changes
that may mean we are starting to listen to someone or something that has been advising the change.

Yes folks, we may now be listening to what or who has persuasively been advising us
that our prior attitudes and beliefs were incompatible with goodness dear mates: that folks is

a good thing isn't it, if indeed the case, it's a good thing that we are turning the corner and
singing spectral serenades aiming for greater heights hoisting the flag of freedom on the mountain
top celebrating with fellow ghosts in our intergalactic realm, rejoicing with one and all
that we are ready to live in the realm in peace and harmony yes with one and all, the noble
goal we set for ourselves through the ages finally realized we seek even higher grounds, to
transform anamorphic to metamorphic states herein in a void, herein this time O yes with
reference to the benevolent forces in the inter-dimensional realm that lead us all
into Eden to perfected perfection yea, that we may yoke with ane, exist in eternal light.

It is fit and proper to congratulate one another and to celebrate our freedom mates:
there is no reason we should not, if even our achievements must be seen as works in progress folks,
for consciousnesses come and go and we are still under threat although we are winning the war yes
against a virus that, reportedly, was 'manufactured' by some ghosts somewhere around yea some wet
market somewhere, which underlines the point we have been making about us being the ghosts tormenting
one another, other ghosts dear mates, so, the ball is in our court to change the trajectory of
our consciousness and make the world a better place for us all dear mates, something we can achieve by
taking decisions on our own to affirm our rights to vote for whoever we choose yes at the
ballot box, in effect, creating the enabling environment for the attainment of the
state of perfection that we seek, one living virtuously in peace and harmony with all assures.